HOPSCOTCH
TWISTY TALES

The Elves
and the
Trendy Shoes

by Evelyn Foster and Claudia Venturini

W
FRANKLIN WATTS
LONDON•SYDNEY

This story is based on the traditional fairy tale,
The Elves and the Shoemaker, but with a new twist.
You can read the original story in
Hopscotch Fairy Tales. Can you make
up your own twist for the story?

First published in 2012 by
Franklin Watts
338 Euston Road
London
NW1 3BH

Franklin Watts Australia
Level 17/207 Kent Street
Sydney
NSW 2000

Text © Evelyn Foster 2012
Illustrations © Claudia Venturini 2012

A CIP catalogue record for this book is available
from the British Library.

ISBN 978 1 4451 0672 4 (hbk)
ISBN 978 1 4451 0678 6 (pbk)

Series Editor: Melanie Palmer
Series Advisor: Catherine Glavina
Series Designer: Peter Scoulding

Printed in China

Franklin Watts is a division of
Hachette Children's Books,
an Hachette UK company
www.hachette.co.uk

For Alina E.F.

The Elves were sad. They were famous
shoemakers, but their shoes had gone
out of fashion in Fairy Tale Land.

The shop bell rang
and Cinderella came in.

"We've made some new glass slippers," said the Elves. Cinderella shook her head. "Oh no, I'm so tired of glass slippers!" she sighed, and left.

The shop bell rang again.

Puss in Boots came in.

"We've made some new boots,"
said the Elves.
Puss in Boots shook his head.
"I'm so bored of boots!" he said,
and marched out again.

The shop bell rang once more.

The Big Bad Wolf came in.

"We've made some fluffy granny slippers," said the Elves.

Wolf shook his head.

"Granny doesn't wear slippers anymore!" he groaned, and left.

The Elves looked at each other sadly.
"Nobody wants our shoes!"
they cried.

They did not notice a shadow
creep past the window.

When they woke the next day, the Elves were shocked. On the floor of their shop were a dozen pairs of new, trendy shoes!

13

The Elves had never seen these kinds of shoes before.
There were high heels,

trendy trainers,

flip flops and smart sandals,

and even a pair
of rollerblades!

Just then the shop door bell rang.

A prince and princess came in.

"What amazing shoes!" they said.
"How unusual! We'd like two pairs
each. Perfect for our royal ball!"

All day long the shoe shop was busy. Soon all the shoes were sold.

"Look at all this gold," said one Elf.

"We're rich!" said the other.

"Who made all the shoes?"
asked one Elf.

"Let's stay up tonight and find out,"
said the other Elf.

So they hid above the shop and
peeped through a hole in the floor.

Then they saw an old man tiptoe into the shop. He was wearing big old boots and he had holes in his clothes. The Elves jumped out!

"I used to be a shoemaker,"
said the man, "but humans got
bored with my shoes. They wanted
something new instead."

Then the Elves had an idea.
"We will give you our fairy tale
shoes. You can sell them in
your shop."

So the Elves sewed the man
some more fairy tale shoes.
In return, the man kept
making modern, trendy shoes
for the Elves.

And all the characters in Fairy Tale Land had the most splendid new shoes at the fancy dress ball!

Puzzle 1

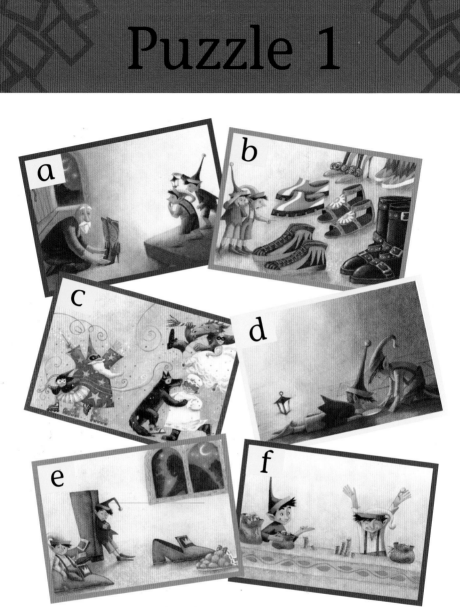

Put these pictures in the correct order.
Which event do you think is most important?
Now try writing the story in your own words!

Puzzle 2

Choose the correct speech bubbles for each character. Can you think of any others? Turn over to find the answers.

Answers

Puzzle 1

The correct order is: 1e, 2b, 3f, 4d, 5a, 6c

Puzzle 2

The Elves: 1, 5

The Shoemaker: 3, 4

Puss in Boots: 2, 6